AR 5.4
pts 1
#171810

THE BEST AUTO RACERS OF ALL TIME

By Barry Wilner

ST. MARY'S PUBLIC LIBRARY
127 Center Street
St. Marys, PA 15857
814 834-6141
email: library@stmaryslibrary.org
www.stmaryslibrary.org

www.abdopublishing.com

Published by Abdo Publishing, a division of ABDO, PO Box 398166, Minneapolis, Minnesota 55439. Copyright © 2015 by Abdo Consulting Group, Inc. International copyrights reserved in all countries. No part of this book may be reproduced in any form without written permission from the publisher. SportsZone™ is a trademark and logo of Abdo Publishing.

Printed in the United States of America, North Mankato, Minnesota
092014
012015

THIS BOOK CONTAINS RECYCLED MATERIALS

Cover Photos: Brian Myrick/AP Images, right; Action Sports Photography/Shutterstock Images, left
Interior Photos: Brian Myrick/AP Images, 1 (right); Action Sports Photography/Shutterstock Images, 1 (left), 15; David Griffin/Icon SMI/Newscom, 7; AP Images, 9, 11, 13, 17, 19, 21, 23, 27, 35, 39; Tom Strickland/AP Images, 25; Charles Kelly/AP Images, 29; Michael Conroy/AP Images, 31; Rene Maestri/AP Images, 33; George Brich/AP Images, 37; Doug Jennings/AP Images, 41; Reed Saxon/AP Images, 43; Chris O'Meara/AP Images, 45; Gilbert Tourte/AP Images, 47; Neftali/Shutterstock Images, 49; Beelde Photography/Shutterstock Images, 51; Doug James/Shutterstock Images, 53; Jacqueline Arzt/AP Images, 55; Remy de la Mauviniere/AP Images, 57; Terry Renna/AP Images, 59; Paul Sancya/AP Images, 61

Editor: Patrick Donnelly
Series Designer: Christa Schneider

Library of Congress Control Number: 2014944202

Cataloging-in-Publication Data
Wilner, Barry.
  The best auto racers of all time / Barry Wilner.
    p. cm. -- (Sports' best ever)
ISBN 978-1-62403-617-0 (lib. bdg.)
Includes bibliographical references and index.
1. Automobile racing--Juvenile literature.   I. Title.
796.72--dc23

2014944202

TABLE OF CONTENTS

Introduction 4
Don Garlits 6
A. J. Foyt 10
Richard Petty 14
Bobby Unser 18
Mario Andretti 22
Al Unser Sr. 26
Jackie Stewart 30
Shirley Muldowney 34
Darrell Waltrip 38
Dale Earnhardt 42
Ayrton Senna 46
Jeff Gordon 50
Michael Schumacher 54
Jimmie Johnson 58

Honorable Mentions 62
Glossary 63
For More Information 63
Index 64
About the Author 64

INTRODUCTION

No matter the sport, fans love speed. And no one goes faster than race car drivers.

Race car drivers are brave. They are strong. They must have sharp eyes and intense concentration. And they have to know every inch of their cars. Drivers race all kinds of superfast vehicles. Some are open-wheel cars. They race in Formula One and IndyCar. Some race stock cars. These NASCAR vehicles are modeled after the cars seen every day on the street. And some race cars are hot rods. They burn down the runways in drag racing. No matter which style, though, all of them are built for speed.

Here are some of the best drivers in auto racing history.

DON GARLITS

Imagine winning the first official race you ever entered. Now imagine you were driving a car that you built. Long before he became known as "Big Daddy," Don Garlits did just that in 1955 at age 23.

Three years later, Garlits moved to the big-time circuit of drag racing. He drove the first of 34 race cars he would nickname "Swamp Rat." Garlits won 144 races overall and 17 season championships, including eight in the NHRA (National Hot Rod Association).

Garlits had many firsts in his career. He was the first man to drive a top fuel dragster to speeds more than 200 mph (322 km/h). He was the first to mount a wing over the engine. Then he became the first driver to go faster than 250 mph (402 km/h). Garlits also developed the first full-body, fire-resistant racing suit. He was a true pioneer.

"Big Daddy" remained a fixture in drag racing for more than 40 years.

"If there hadn't been a Don Garlits, maybe there wouldn't have been an NHRA," said John Force, another great drag racer.

Garlits raced for more than 40 years. He loved the speed, the competition, and the way his dragsters shook the ground as their noisy engines fired up.

"I liked the idea of two cars lined up side by side, not bumping into one another," he said. "It was one person against one person, one machine against one machine. There was a winner and a loser."

In 1970, Garlits's car exploded in a race in Long Beach, California. He was so badly injured that he lost part of his right foot. The crash inspired Big Daddy to design a dragster with the engine in the back to help keep drivers safer in crashes. Soon he was back on the track, winning more races.

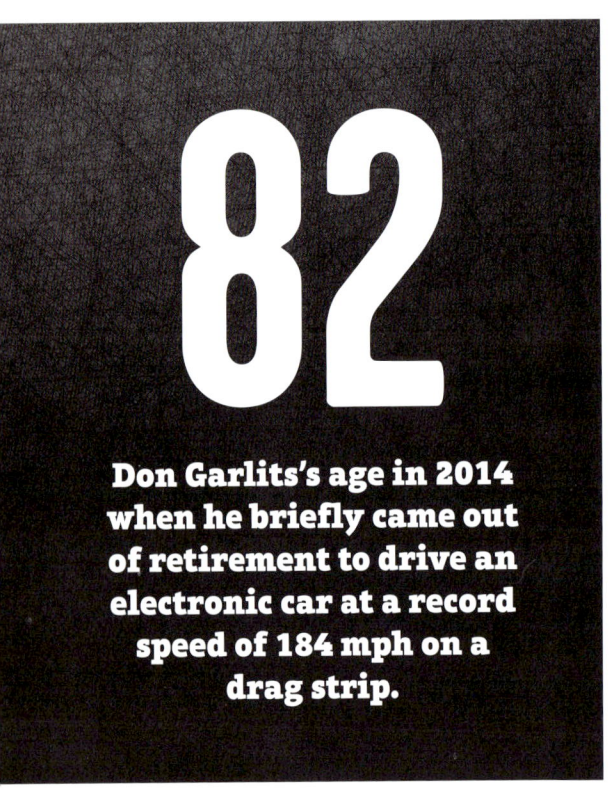

82

Don Garlits's age in 2014 when he briefly came out of retirement to drive an electronic car at a record speed of 184 mph on a drag strip.

Don Garlits had plenty of opportunities to celebrate at the finish line.

DON GARLITS

Hometown: Tampa, Florida
Birth Date: January 14, 1932
Race Circuit: NHRA (1958–2003)
Race Wins: 144
Series Championships: 17

A. J. FOYT

No matter what kind of race car A. J. Foyt drove or owned, he was a winner.

For nearly 60 years, Anthony Joseph Foyt Jr.—A. J. to just about everybody—earned checkered flags. His four Indianapolis 500 victories were tied for the most ever through 2014. And nobody had matched his seven series championships.

But Foyt loved challenges. So he also drove in other series. He drove in 29 NASCAR races and won seven. He raced in three Formula One events. Plus he competed in the famous 24 Hours of LeMans in France. He won that sports car endurance race in 1967.

Foyt is the only racer to have won the Indy 500, the Daytona 500, and the LeMans. He retired as a driver in 1993. But he did not stop competing. As a car owner, Foyt has won two IndyCar championships. He entered the Motorsports Hall of Fame in 2000.

A. J. Foyt is all smiles after winning his first Indianapolis 500 in 1961.

Was it all fun for Foyt? Yes, but it was also scary.

"Every race I ever ran, at one time or another I scared myself to death," Foyt said. "You hear these guys saying they never scared (themselves). Well, maybe they're a lot braver than A. J. Foyt. But there probably wasn't a race that went by that I didn't thrill myself."

That was true from the beginning, when Foyt competed at small dirt tracks in sprint and midget cars. He especially loved racing at the Indianapolis Motor Speedway. So he came out of retirement in 1994 when NASCAR ran its first race at the famous speedway. Foyt finished thirtieth and then became a full-time owner.

35

The record number of Indianapolis 500s in a row in which A. J. Foyt drove, from 1958 to 1992. He won it four times (1961, 1964, 1967, 1977).

A. J. Foyt takes the checkered flag at the 1977 Indianapolis 500, his record-setting fourth win in the event.

A. J. FOYT

Hometown: Houston, Texas
Birth Date: January 16, 1935
Race Circuits: IndyCar (1957–93), NASCAR (1963–94)
Race Wins: 74 (67 IndyCar, 7 NASCAR)
Series Championships: 7 (IndyCar: 1960, 1961, 1963, 1964, 1967, 1975, 1979)
Indianapolis 500 wins: 4 (1961, 1964, 1967, 1977)
Daytona 500 win: 1 (1972)

RICHARD PETTY

From dirt tracks on Wednesday nights to superspeedways on Sunday afternoons, Richard Petty was the man to beat. He won 200 races during his career. Only one driver in NASCAR history has won half as many through 2014. Sometimes Petty's cars seemed to be held together by tape and wire. But he would still take the checkered flag.

Petty came from a racing family. His father, Lee, won two NASCAR championships. And his son, Kyle, won eight races. At first, Richard was not behind the wheel. He and his older brother, Maurice, worked on the crew for their dad. Lee told Richard he had to be 21 years old before he could race.

"The King" flashed his smile in victory lane a record 200 times.

When Richard finally turned 21, Lee gave him an older car to race in local events. Soon, Richard was driving in the same races as his dad. He was NASCAR Rookie of the Year in 1959. However, he did not get his first win until February 28, 1960. It came on a dirt track in Charlotte, North Carolina. In fact, his dad helped him win by bumping another car late in the race. That cleared the way for Richard.

Soon, Petty was winning everywhere. It did not matter what type of car he drove. He won 138 times in a Plymouth. But he had wins in six other models too. Petty was soon known as "The King." His success in his famous No. 43 car helped make NASCAR popular nationwide. It is no surprise he ended up in the NASCAR Hall of Fame.

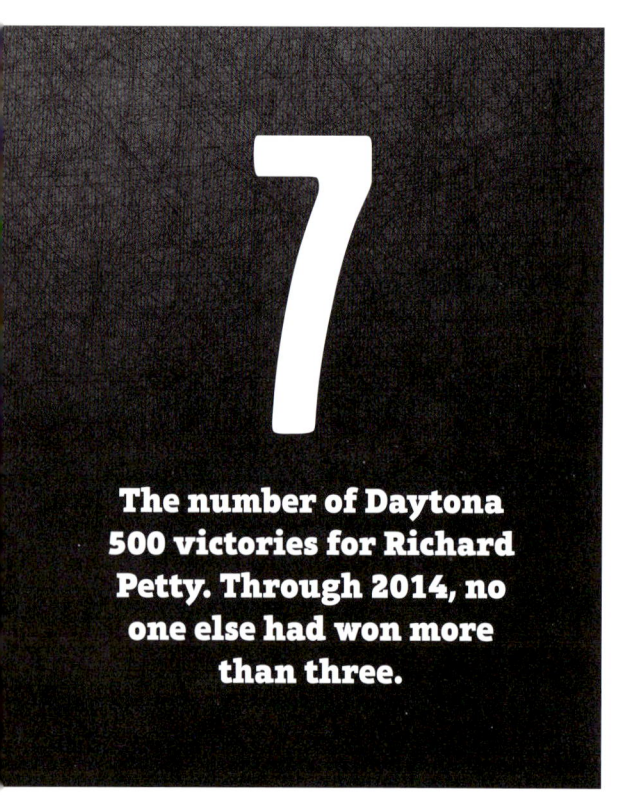

7

The number of Daytona 500 victories for Richard Petty. Through 2014, no one else had won more than three.

Richard Petty and his No. 43 car formed the most dominant team in NASCAR history.

RICHARD PETTY

Hometown: Randleman, North Carolina

Birth Date: July 2, 1937

Race Circuit: NASCAR (1958–92)

Race Wins: 200

Series Championships: 7 (1964, 1967, 1971, 1972, 1974, 1975, 1979)

Daytona 500 wins: 7 (1964, 1966, 1971, 1973, 1974, 1979, 1981)

BOBBY UNSER

Bobby Unser liked going fast, but only in automobiles. He often drove them 200 mph (322 km/h) or faster. But he hated flying. Unser was afraid of heights. He did not like being scared, though. So midway through his 19 seasons in racing, Unser became a pilot. As he once said, "I will go fast until the day I die."

Unser was only 15 years old when he won his first title as a driver. Driving his father's car, he won a road race in Mexico. Soon, he had switched to open wheels. He was on his way to a Hall of Fame career.

The Unsers are one of auto racing's most successful families. Bobby was the first Unser to win the Indianapolis 500. That race had not been kind to the family. Bobby's older brother, Jerry, had died in a crash while preparing for the Indy 500 in 1959.

Bobby Unser waves to his fans at the 1971 Indianapolis 500.

Bobby became the first driver to win the Indianapolis 500 in three different decades. He won in 1968, 1975, and 1981. But his last victory was not official for months. Unser had the fastest car, won the pole, and led nearly the whole race. But officials said he passed some cars under a caution. That is not allowed. He finished eight seconds in front of Mario Andretti. However, Unser was penalized and Andretti was made the winner.

Unser appealed the decision. Eventually, he was given the trophy. It was his final victory. He retired from racing at the end of the year.

9

The number of Indianapolis 500s won by the Unser family. Bobby won three, his brother Al Sr. won four, and Al Jr. won two.

Bobby Unser celebrates his third Indy 500. He soon was stripped of the title, but he won on appeal.

BOBBY UNSER

Hometown: Albuquerque, New Mexico
Birth Date: February 20, 1934
Race Circuit: IndyCar (1963–81)
Race Wins: 37
Series Championships: 2 (1968, 1974)
Indianapolis 500 wins: 3 (1968, 1975, 1981)

MARIO ANDRETTI

If you are looking for Mario Andretti at a race track, you should probably start your search in victory lane.

Andretti raced open-wheel vehicles in IndyCar and Formula One. He also drove stock cars in NASCAR. Wherever he was, Andretti usually was the man to beat. He won 65 races in his career. He is the only driver to have won the Daytona 500, the Indianapolis 500, and a Formula One season championship. Through 2014, he also was the last American to win a Formula One race. He did so in 1978, when he won six races and the season title.

Mario Andretti waves from the winner's circle after winning the 1969 Indianapolis 500.

Andretti is the head of a successful racing family. His son Michael is a top open-wheel driver. His grandson Marco also is a successfully IndyCar driver. But the elder Andretti remains the greatest racer in the family. He could win in all types of cars and on all kinds of tracks.

"I went where the action was, from sports cars to dirt to Indy, then maybe off to Argentina for Formula One," Mario said.

Andretti's family spent seven years in an Italian refugee camp after World War II. They often lived with little food or comfort. They came to the United States by ship when he was 15. They settled in Pennsylvania, and, soon after, Andretti was racing cars. And he was winning.

When Andretti was done behind the wheel, he explored other interests. In 1996 he opened an award-winning winery in California's Napa Valley. It was a good fit for Andretti, who has grown used to winning.

5

Number of times in 29 Indianapolis 500 races that Andretti finished all 500 miles.

Mario Andretti, *left*, gives advice to his son, Michael, before a practice round at the 2001 Indianapolis 500.

MARIO ANDRETTI

Hometown: Nazareth, Pennsylvania

Birth Date: February 28, 1940

Race Circuits: NASCAR (1966–69), Formula One (1968–1982), IndyCar (1979–94)

Race Wins: 65 (52 IndyCar, 12 Formula One, 1 NASCAR)

Series Championships: 5
IndyCar (1965, 1966, 1969, 1984)
Formula One (1978)

Indianapolis 500 win: 1 (1969)

Daytona 500 win: 1 (1967)

AL UNSER SR.

Racing has always been a family affair for the Unsers. The first victory of Al Unser Sr.'s racing career came in a car built by his father, Jerry, and his older brother Bobby. By the time Al was done competing, he had 39 victories, including four Indianapolis 500s. Through 2014, nobody had won that race more often. He also had seen his son, Al Jr., rise to the top of IndyCar.

Unser had a few bumps in the road along the way. In 1969, for example, he broke his ankle while riding a motorcycle. When it healed, he got back behind the wheel. He won five times the rest of that season.

Unser's records include being the only driver through 2014 to win the Triple Crown of 500-mile races in a season. In 1978, he won at Indianapolis, Pocono, and Ontario. He also was the first racer to win the Indy 500 in consecutive years.

Al Unser Sr., celebrates with his wife, Karen, after he tied A. J. Foyt's record by winning his fourth Indianapolis 500.

One of Unser's championships was harder to celebrate than the rest.

In the final race of the 1985 season, Al Sr. finished fourth as Al Jr. came in third. Still, that was enough for the father to beat the son by one point for the IndyCar season title.

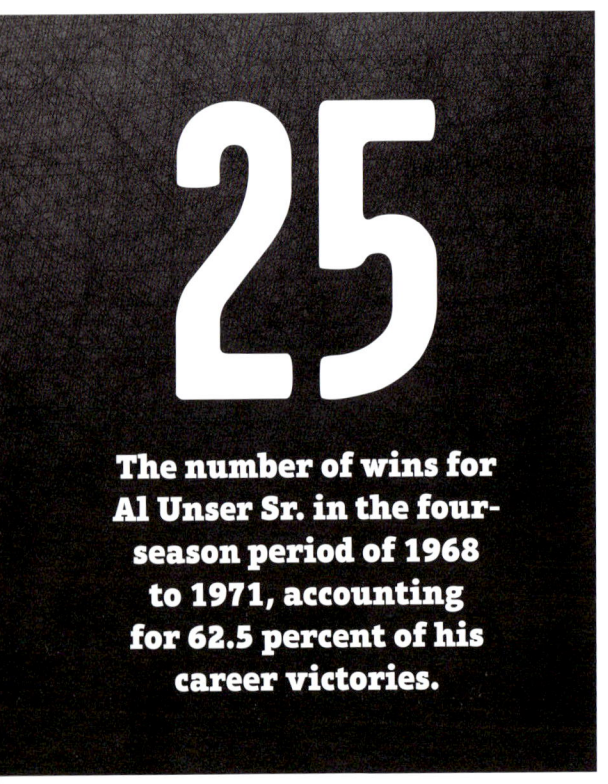

The number of wins for Al Unser Sr. in the four-season period of 1968 to 1971, accounting for 62.5 percent of his career victories.

Unser's fourth Indy 500 win was the strangest. At age 47, he went to Indianapolis not knowing if he would have a car to race. When driver Danny Ongais got injured in practice, Al Sr. took his spot in the race. And he zoomed off to his final victory, thrilling everyone, especially Al Jr.

"They called him retired and washed up and all that," Al Jr. said. "He's far from that. I've got goose bumps. I'm ecstatic for Dad."

Al Unser Sr., *right*, chats with his brother Bobby and their mother at the Indianapolis Motor Speedway in 1965.

AL UNSER SR.

Hometown: Albuquerque, New Mexico
Birth Date: May 29, 1939
Race Circuit: IndyCar (1964–94)
Race Wins: 39
Series Championships: 3 (1970, 1983, 1985)
Indianapolis 500 wins: 4 (1970, 1971, 1978, 1987)

JACKIE STEWART

Jackie Stewart grew up in Scotland, where his father owned a garage.

Jackie's mother did not want him or his older brother, Jimmy, to race. But Jackie was a great driver. He also had many problems in school because of a learning disorder. He found it hard to pay attention in school. But he had much more success behind the wheel of a car. Soon he was racing full-time. Stewart began winning races, taking seven straight in the minor-league British F-3 series in 1963. By 1965, he was a regular in Formula One.

When he joined Team Tyrrell, Stewart became the top contender at nearly every track, road, and street course where Formula One competed. By 1969, he was on top of the standings. He won six races that year—a career high.

Jackie Stewart leads a parade of bagpipers before the start of the US Grand Prix at Indianapolis Motor Speedway in 2004.

While becoming a champion in Formula One, Stewart also was pushing for safety measures for the cars and drivers. Some people said he was taking away the excitement and glamour of racing. That angered Stewart.

"They said I had no guts. But not many of these critics had ever crashed at 150 miles an hour," Stewart said.

Stewart even tried IndyCar, racing twice in the Indianapolis 500. He was leading in 1966 when mechanical trouble forced him to drop out with only nine laps left. But he was still chosen as the race's top rookie. The next year, he was close to the leaders when his engine failed late in the race.

After he stopped driving, Stewart became a TV analyst and a race team owner. He also continued to push for safer cars and race tracks.

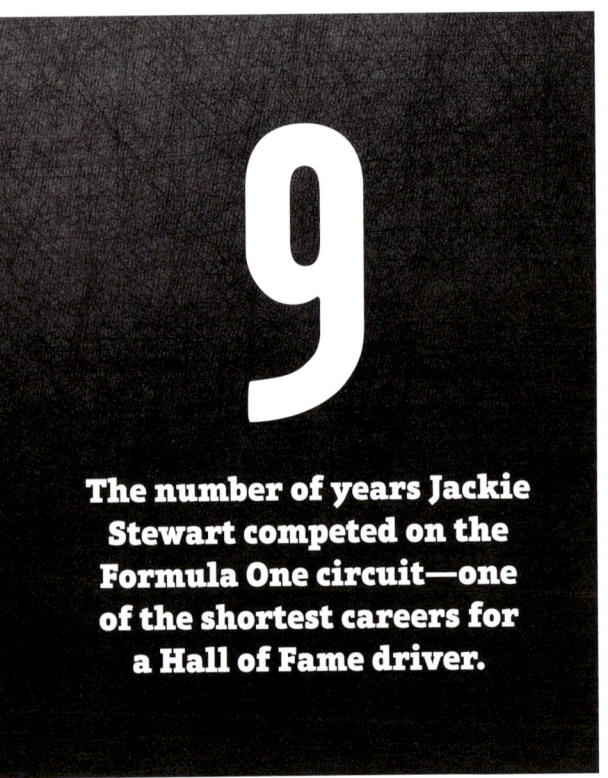

9

The number of years Jackie Stewart competed on the Formula One circuit—one of the shortest careers for a Hall of Fame driver.

Jackie Stewart crosses the finish line first in his Tyrrell Ford to win the Monaco Grand Prix in 1973.

JACKIE STEWART

Hometown: Milton, Scotland
Birth Date: June 11, 1939
Race Circuit: Formula One (1965–73)
Race Wins: 27
Series Championships: 3 (1969, 1971, 1973)

SHIRLEY MULDOWNEY

Shirley Muldowney never understood why people thought women could not compete against men in sports. So she went out and proved they could, in championship style.

Muldowney was the first great female drag racer. In 1973, she became the first woman to earn a top fuel license. Top fuel cars are the fastest race cars at any level. Then she began beating men at the highest level. In 1977, she won the NHRA championship. She did it again in 1980 and 1982. That made her the first person, male or female, with three top fuel titles.

But Muldowney was more than just a great racer. She was a true trailblazer. These days, women compete in all forms of racing, from Danica Patrick in NASCAR to Ashley Force Hood in the NHRA. And Muldowney paved the way for them.

Shirley Muldowney was the "First Lady of Drag Racing" and a role model for women who wanted to get behind the wheel.

One of Muldowney's biggest challenges came in 1984. Her front tire blew, and her dragster veered into a ditch at 250 mph (402 km/h). The crash broke both of her legs. It was months before she could walk again.

But she returned to the track in 1986 and was awarded the Comeback Driver of the Year honor. Her last victory was in 1989 at the Fall Nationals.

Muldowney never liked her nickname, "Cha Cha." She eventually said she preferred to be called the "First Lady of Drag Racing." In 1983, the film *Heart Like a Wheel* earned actress Bonnie Bedelia a Golden Globe nomination for her portrayal of Muldowney.

"I'd love to drive again," Muldowney said in 2009. "And I could. I know I could drive like I always could. But the opportunity isn't there for me, so I retired. And I am only going to say that once."

18

The number of races Shirley Muldowney won. Her impact as the first great woman driver makes her an all-time great.

Shirley Muldowney was the first woman licensed by the NHRA to drive top fuel dragsters.

SHIRLEY MULDOWNEY

Hometown: Burlington, Vermont
Birth Date: June 19, 1940
Race Circuit: NHRA (1965–2003)
Race Wins: 18
Series Championships: 3 (1977, 1980, 1982)

DARRELL WALTRIP

Darrell Waltrip has become famous for what he has to say about racing. In fact, his voice has made him almost as famous as his driving. Waltrip is a three-time Cup Series champion, with 84 career wins. He is also the unofficial "Voice of NASCAR" for his TV announcing, which he took up after retiring as a driver.

While Waltrip enjoys calling races, he wants to be remembered most for the way he handled a car. When he entered the NASCAR Hall of Fame in 2012, Waltrip recalled advice he got along the way: "They always told me, if you're going to dream, dream as big as you possibly can because you know what, it might just come true. And tonight, I'm living proof of that."

Darrell Waltrip took home the trophy at the Rebel 500 at Darlington Raceway in 1979.

Waltrip proved himself first on short tracks around the country. When he finally raced on the 2.5-mile (4 km) superspeedway at Daytona, he did not have as much success. He joked that his wife, Stevie, figured out the problem halfway through the race. Darrell was hungry. He had never driven in such a long race.

But Waltrip soon mastered every size track. When he won the Daytona 500 for the only time in 1989, he jumped up and down and danced in the winner's circle like a little kid. He kept shouting, "I won the Daytona 500!"

Waltrip was not the most popular driver in the early 1970s. Richard Petty once told him he had to calm down to keep everyone happy, especially the car sponsors and the fans. Waltrip did, and now he is as popular as any of the drivers he talks about on TV.

12

Darrell Waltrip won 12 times at Bristol Motor Speedway, a short track often called "The Bullring." He won seven straight races there from 1981 to 1984.

Darrell Waltrip celebrates after finally winning the Daytona 500 in 1989.

DARRELL WALTRIP

Hometown: Owensboro, Kentucky
Birth Date: February 5, 1947
Race Circuit: NASCAR (1972–2000)
Cup Race Wins: 84
Series Championships: 3 (1981, 1982, 1985)
Daytona 500 win: 1 (1989)

DALE EARNHARDT

Fans called Dale Earnhardt "The Intimidator." That is because drivers never wanted to see Earnhardt's black No. 3 Chevrolet behind them.

Cars are usually close together in a NASCAR race. Near the end of a race, drivers think about one thing: winning. If it means tapping another car to move it out of the way, well, that is what has to be done. And no one was better at it than Earnhardt. He won seven Cup Series championships. That was tied for the most with Richard Petty through 2014.

"Second place is just the first-place loser," Earnhardt often said.

The steely glare of Dale Earnhardt, a.k.a. "The Intimidator"

It took Earnhardt 20 years to finally win the Daytona 500. After that victory in 1998, members of the pit crews from nearly every other team showed their respect. They waited in pit row to slap hands with "The Intimidator."

Earnhardt was killed in a crash near the end of the Daytona 500 in 2001. Michael Waltrip, Earnhardt's teammate, won his first race in 463 tries that day. Earnhardt's son, Dale Jr., finished second. Dale Sr. helped them by blocking other cars from passing on the final laps. But in the last turn, his car was tapped and went directly into the wall.

After Earnhardt's death, NASCAR made many changes to the cars and the race tracks to increase safety. Through 2014, no other driver had died in a Cup race. Safety improvements are not Earnhardt's only legacy, though. His son, Dale Jr., has gone on to become NASCAR's most popular driver.

From 2001 to 2014, the No. 3 car was retired from Cup racing by its owner, Richard Childress. Childress's grandson, Austin Dillon, brought it back in 2014.

Dale Earnhardt is ecstatic after winning his first, and only, Daytona 500 in 1998.

DALE EARNHARDT

Hometown: Kannapolis, North Carolina
Birth Date: April 29, 1951
Race Circuit: NASCAR (1975–2001)
Race Wins: 76
Series Championships: 7 (1980, 1986, 1987, 1990, 1991, 1993, 1994)
Daytona 500 win: 1 (1998)

AYRTON SENNA

Until the day he died, Ayrton Senna fought for improved safety in Formula One cars. In fact, shortly before his death he was troubled when Formula One passed new rules that took away many electronic driving aids. The International Auto Racing Federation wanted to give the drivers more control of the cars. On the night before his final race at the San Marino Grand Prix in 1994, Senna even wrote an article saying he was worried.

"My car reacts a bit nervously on this kind of race surface," he wrote. Just hours later, Senna was dead at age 34.

Senna was one of the most exciting drivers Formula One has ever seen. He was very popular in his native Brazil. Newspapers there reported his death as if he were a national hero.

Ayrton Senna was one of the most exciting and successful drivers in Formula One history.

One of Senna's specialties was winning poles. He grabbed 65 of them to set a record, though Michael Schumacher later broke it. Senna was a master at getting his car to top speed and keeping it there. He raced for a company, Team McLaren, that did not always have the fastest cars. Yet in 1988, 1990, and 1991, Senna was the Formula One champion. He proved he did not always need the speediest vehicle to take the checkered flag.

Senna was a winner from the time he began racing go-karts when he was four years old. He also launched his own comic book, and he loved to play tennis and fly model airplanes. Many of today's top Formula One drivers list Senna as one of their biggest racing heroes.

556

The number of laps out of 895 raced that Ayrton Senna led in 1990—an amazing 62 percent.

Ayrton Senna was so popular in his native Brazil that his image was used for a postage stamp after his death.

AYRTON SENNA

Hometown: Sao Paulo, Brazil
Birth Date: March 21, 1960
Race Circuit: Formula One (1984–94)
Race Wins: 41
Series Championships: 3 (1988, 1990, 1991)

JEFF GORDON

When he came onto the NASCAR scene, Jeff Gordon was called "Wonder Boy." After 10 years of racing and four Cup Series titles, people called him "The Champ." After more than 20 years behind the wheel of a stock car, some of Gordon's fellow drivers could call him "Old Man."

Although only 11 of Gordon's 92 wins came between 2008 and 2014, he remains one of NASCAR's most popular athletes. He often is the first person his fellow drivers go to for advice. He is known for taking a stand when he sees a problem on the track. And he speaks up when the racing becomes too dangerous or drivers are taking too many risks.

Through 2014, Jeff Gordon had won 92 races and had at least nine victories at each of the three types of NASCAR courses.

Gordon has always been known for his "car control." That means he can drive any vehicle well on any track. Gordon has won on every kind of track. Through 2014, he had 29 victories on superspeedways, which are 2 miles (3.2 km) or longer. He also had won 16 races on short tracks, which are less than 1 mile (1.6 km) long. And nine of his wins had come on road courses.

After Gordon barely edged his teammate, Jimmie Johnson, in a 2011 race, Johnson was not angry to have lost. "He may not have had the dominance that we'd seen before, but it's still Jeff Gordon," Johnson said. "And it's so cool to race that hard with him."

Gordon also is a champion fundraiser. In recent years, he has driven a car sponsored by Drive to End Hunger. He has helped raise millions of dollars to help that cause. The organization has fought to end adult hunger and donated more than 20 million meals.

13

The number of wins Jeff Gordon had in 1998. Through 2014, that remained the most by one driver in a season in NASCAR's modern era (post-1972).

Jeff Gordon, *right*, chats with his teammate and rival Jimmie Johnson.

JEFF GORDON

Hometown: Vallejo, California
Birth Date: August 4, 1971
Race Circuit: NASCAR (1990–)
Race Wins: 92*
Series Championships: 4 (1995, 1997, 1998, 2001)*
Daytona 500 wins: 3 (1997, 1999, 2005)*
*Through 2014

MICHAEL SCHUMACHER

Certain athletes have dominated individual sports. In golf, there was Tiger Woods. In tennis, there was Roger Federer. And in auto racing, their equal in the same era was Michael Schumacher. He was known for his hard-charging style of driving. When Schumacher retired from Formula One racing, he had 91 wins. The next closest racer was Alain Prost with 51. Schumacher also had seven season championships—two more than anyone else.

Schumacher's career began slowly, with just two wins in his first three seasons. But once he got his Benetton team rolling in 1994, Schumacher was almost unbeatable. When he won his first series title that year, he was not even on the track. Schumacher and Damon Hill crashed and were knocked out of the final race in Australia. But Schumacher had dominated enough earlier in the season to still win.

Michael Schumacher relaxes in front of a large photo of himself at Silverstone race track in England in 1996.

Schumacher later switched to Ferrari, one of the biggest names in auto racing. From 2000 to 2004, he was unstoppable. He won 48 races in those five championship seasons. The German star considered 2002 his greatest season. That year, he finished in the top four in all 17 races.

It did not matter to "Schumi," as his friends called him, where the races occurred. He won Formula One races on the streets of Monte Carlo, Monaco. He won on the road course at the Indianapolis Motor Speedway. And he won on every continent where the circuit raced. Sebastian Vettel, now the top driver in Formula One, often has said that Schumacher was his idol.

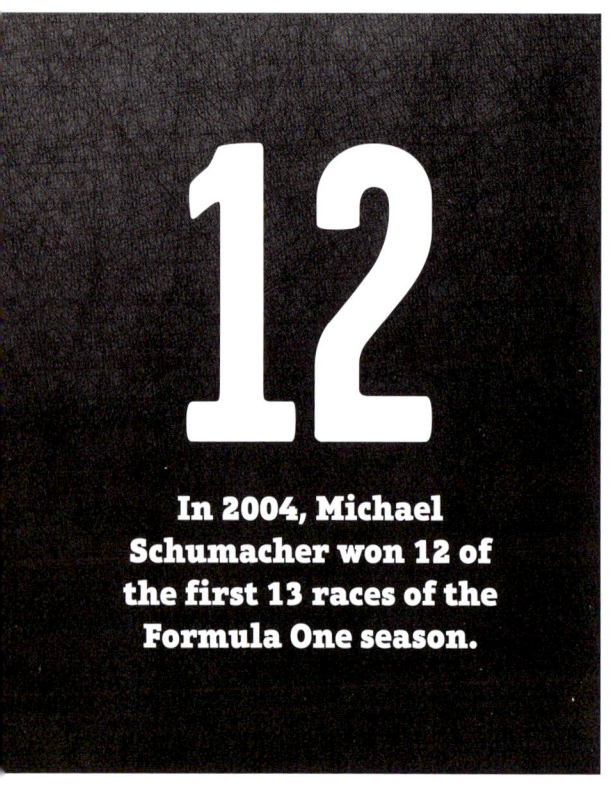

In 2004, Michael Schumacher won 12 of the first 13 races of the Formula One season.

Few people have dominated a sport the way Michael Schumacher dominated Formula One throughout his career.

MICHAEL SCHUMACHER

Hometown: Hurth Hermulheim, Germany

Birth Date: January 3, 1969

Race Circuit: Formula One (1991–2012)

Race Wins: 91

Series Championships: 7 (1994, 1995, 2000, 2001, 2002, 2003, 2004)

JIMMIE JOHNSON

Jimmie Johnson was driving in NASCAR's second-level series and not winning many races. Then Jeff Gordon, already a three-time Cup Series champion, showed up at Darlington Raceway. Gordon saw this young driver handling "the track too tough to tame" with ease. He was impressed with Johnson's skill behind the wheel.

Gordon's car owner, Rick Hendrick, wanted to start a fourth team. Gordon recommended Johnson for the ride. Gordon even became part owner of the Lowe's 48 racing team that Johnson took over in 2002. It is safe to say that neither man regrets the decision.

Since Johnson joined Hendrick Motorsports, he has piled up the championships. Through 2014, he had won six Cup Series titles. He also had won races at 18 of the 22 tracks on the NASCAR circuit.

Jimmie Johnson is one of the most recognizable faces in NASCAR today.

As of 2014, Johnson's Hendrick Motorsports teammates were some of the top names in racing, including Gordon, Dale Earnhardt Jr., and Kasey Kahne.

One reason for Johnson's success has been his skill at finding "racing grooves." Those are the fastest spots on each track. Another is his patience. Johnson often will move steadily through the pack of cars. He knows he does not need to rush to the front. He trusts that his skill will help him pull ahead at the end. And he is usually right.

Johnson has been with the same crew chief, Chad Knaus, for his whole career. Their relationship has given them a winning edge because they communicate so well. "I think we . . . realize that it's okay to ask hard questions if you believe the answer you're going to get," Knaus said.

5

No driver had won more than two straight NASCAR championships before Jimmie Johnson won five in a row from 2006 to 2010.

Jimmie Johnson, *right*, chats with crew chief Chad Knaus. Johnson credits much of his success to their partnership.

JIMMIE JOHNSON

Hometown: El Cajon, California
Birth Date: September 17, 1975
Race Circuit: NASCAR (1998–)
Race Wins: 70*
Series Championships: 6 (2006, 2007, 2008, 2009, 2010, 2013)*
Daytona 500 wins: 2 (2006, 2013)*
* Through 2014

HONORABLE MENTIONS

Bobby Allison – The 1983 Cup champion won 84 races, including three Daytona 500s, and was elected to the NASCAR Hall of Fame in 2011.

Emerson Fittipaldi – The versatile Brazilian won 14 F1 races, two series titles, two Indy 500s, and the 1989 IndyCar championship. He made the International Motorsports Hall of Fame in 2003.

John Force – Force had 16 drag racing funny car championships and 141 wins through 2014. He was inducted into the International Motorsports Hall of Fame in 2012.

Junior Johnson – The 1960 Daytona 500 champion also won 132 races and six Cup Series titles as an owner. He also made the NASCAR Hall of Fame in 2010.

Niki Lauda – The Austrian won three Formula One titles and won 25 times in 171 races. He entered the International Motorsports Hall of Fame in 1993.

Rick Mears – One of the great American open-wheel drivers, Mears took four Indy 500s and three series titles. He also made the International Motorsports Hall of Fame in 1997.

David Pearson – Second only to Richard Petty with 105 NASCAR wins, Pearson took three Cup Series crowns and won the 1976 Daytona 500. He made the NASCAR Hall of Fame in 2011.

Alain Prost – The French star made the International Motorsports Hall of Fame in 1999, following four Formula One championships and a record-setting 51 wins.

Johnny Rutherford – A dominant racer for a decade, Rutherford won the Indy 500 in 1974, 1976, and 1980, and he joined the International Motorsports Hall of Fame in 1996.

Tony Stewart – The three-time NASCAR Cup champion also won a title in open-wheel racing in the Indy Racing League in 1997, and he owns a sprint car racing team.

GLOSSARY

caution period
A time when drivers must slow down because the track has become unsafe due to an accident, debris, or bad weather.

checkered flag
A flag of black-and-white squares waved when the winner crosses the finish line.

open wheel
Refers to any type of race car in which the car's wheels sit outside its body.

pit
The area where cars come in for fuel, tires, adjustments, and repairs during on-track sessions.

pole position
The first car in line at the start of a race.

rookie
A first-year driver in a circuit.

series
A set of races in which riders compete throughout a season.

sponsor
A business or other organization that covers the expenses of a driving team.

stock car
A standard car that is modified for racing.

FOR MORE INFORMATION

Further Readings

Arute, Jack. *Jack Arute's Tales from the Indianapolis 500*. Champaign, IL: Sports Publishing LLC, 2012.

Long, Dustin. *The Daytona 500*. Minneapolis, MN: Abdo Publishing Co., 2013.

Young, Jeff C. *Dropping the Flag: Auto Racing*. Minneapolis, MN: Abdo Publishing Co., 2011.

Websites

To learn more about Sports' Best Ever, visit **booklinks.abdopublishing.com**. These links are routinely monitored and updated to provide the most current information available.

INDEX

Andretti, Mario, 20, 22, 24–25
Andretti, Michael, 24

Bristol Motor Speedway, 40

Childress, Richard, 44

Darlington Raceway, 58
Daytona 500, 10, 16, 22, 40, 44
Dillon, Austin, 44

Earnhardt, Dale Jr., 44, 60
Earnhardt, Dale Sr., 42, 44–45

Force, John, 8
Formula One, 5, 10, 22, 24, 30, 32, 46, 48, 54, 56
Foyt, A. J., 10, 12–13

Garlits, Don, 6, 8–9
Gordon, Jeff, 50, 52–53, 58, 60

Hendrick, Rick, 58, 60

Hill, Damon, 54
Hood, Ashley Force, 34

Indianapolis 500, 10, 12, 18, 20, 22, 24, 26, 28, 32
Indianapolis Motor Speedway, 12, 56
IndyCar, 5, 10, 22, 24, 26, 28, 32

Johnson, Jimmie, 52, 58, 60–61

Kahne, Kasey, 60
Knaus, Chad, 60

Muldowney, Shirley, 34, 36–37

NASCAR, 5, 10, 12, 14, 16, 22, 34, 38, 42, 44, 50, 52, 58, 60
NHRA, 6, 8, 34

Ongais, Danny, 28

Patrick, Danica, 34
Petty, Lee, 14, 16
Petty, Maurice, 14
Petty, Richard, 14, 16–17, 40, 42
Prost, Alain, 54

San Marino Grand Prix, 46
Schumacher, Michael, 48, 54, 56–57
Senna, Ayrton, 46, 48–49
Stewart, Jackie, 30, 32–33

24 Hours of LeMans, 10

Unser, Al Jr., 20, 26, 28
Unser, Al Sr., 20, 26, 28–29
Unser, Bobby, 18, 20–21, 26
Unser, Jerry Jr., 18
Unser, Jerry Sr., 26

Vettel, Sebastian, 56

Waltrip, Darrell, 38, 40–41
Waltrip, Michael, 44

ABOUT THE AUTHOR

Barry Wilner has been a sportswriter with the Associated Press since 1976 and has covered the Super Bowl, the Olympics, the World Cup, the Pan American Games, the Stanley Cup, and many other sporting events. He has written more than 40 books. Wilner lives in Garnerville, New York.

$22.95
1-16

T 580054